TO:

Dear Brinna

Hi Aunty

For Joe Buffalo Stuart with all my heart. Get well.

British Library Cataloguing in Publication Data
Stuart, Alexander
    Joe, Jo-Jo and the monkey masks.
    I. Title   II. Vendrell, Carme Solé
    823'.914[J]   PZ7
    ISBN 0–86264–199–3

Text © 1988 by Alexander Stuart. Illustrations © 1988 by Carme Solé Vendrell. First
published in 1988 by Andersen Press Ltd., 62–65 Chandos Place, London WC2.
Published in Australia by Century Hutchinson Australia Pty. Ltd.,
16–22 Church Street, Hawthorn, Victoria 3122. All rights reserved. Colour
separated by Photolitho AG Offsetreproduktionen, Gossau, Zürich, Switzerland.
Printed in Italy by Grafiche AZ, Verona.

Joe, Jo-Jo and the Monkey Masks

Story by Alexander Stuart
Pictures by Carme Solé Vendrell

Andersen Press · London

Hutchinson · Australia

It was a hot day when Joe and Jo-Jo took their parents to the zoo. The sun beat down, bang, bang, and made the zoo seem a foreign place, filled with the squawks and shrieks and trumpetings of a dream. It was a day when an ice cream would melt in 2 seconds all over your hand. It was a day to run wild, which is what Joe and Jo-Jo did.

They got up to all kinds of monkey tricks, so their mummy bought them both monkey masks.

When it was time to leave, Joe and Jo-Jo took the monkey masks off their own faces and put them on their mummy and daddy.

And Mummy and Daddy started playing games, making monkey noises and bouncing up and down, so that when they got to the car, other drivers were astonished to see two monkeys in the company of two children – and one of the monkeys driving.

Back home, bananas for tea did seem a little unusual, but Joe and Jo-Jo gladly helped out when Daddy started ripping wallpaper off the walls and Mummy jumped up on top of the fridge. As they all ripped and tore, sharp, savage leaves poked through into the room and strange, musky scents filled the air.

Suddenly, their home looked like a jungle. Parrots came to roost in the eaves, where the sparrows had been. Tall grass grew up in front of their eyes, covering the carpet. And the fridge hummed and whirred, filled to bursting with a monstrous hoard of bananas.

At first, Joe and Jo-Jo felt content and excited in the heat of the sun. But when they tried to speak to their parents, Daddy only grunted "Uh-uh-uh-uh!" and Mummy sat them down and started picking through their hair for fleas.

Jo-Jo phoned the zoo and asked for an expert to come round fast. When the expert arrived, he professed bafflement at what had happened.

"I observe something very curious about your parents," he explained, speaking through his nose as experts commonly do. "They look like monkeys. They behave like monkeys. They even decorate their home like monkeys. Clearly they have convinced themselves that they *are* monkeys. Who are we to argue with that?"

And when he went to fetch a second opinion, the professor he brought back with him needed a machete just to get near Joe and Jo-Jo's home.

For the jungle which had begun in their living room had spread at an alarming rate. Their neighbours' houses were gone, vanished under a dark tangle of vegetation. And their neighbours – their neighbours were monkeys too! Menacing growls came from where the newsagent's had once been. A magnificent lion now guarded what was left of the milkman's float.

The second professor professed his ignorance.

"This is so unusual," he said, as he glanced nervously in the direction of the lion, "that we have no words to describe it. In fact," he observed, jumping into the first professor's arms, "the only words which come to mind are – GOODBYE!"

And Joe and Jo-Jo were left alone. Alone with a lot of monkeys.

As far as they could see, in every direction, stretched a world that was wild and unknowable. They wanted to hug their parents for comfort, but when they did, they were swept high up into the trees and had to cling on for dear life.

Then they felt more frightened than ever.

"I want to go home," Joe told his mother.

"So do I," Jo-Jo said to her father.

"WE WANT TO GO HOME!" they howled.

Their parents stared at them with worried monkey eyes.

"Uh!" said their daddy, trying hard to speak.

"Uh-uh-uh!" cried their mummy, sounding almost human.

And as the branches swayed and swung, and Joe and Jo-Jo gripped their parents tight, they leapt out of the trees and landed with a jolt.

"But this is home," their mummy said.

"Don't you recognise the mess?" asked their daddy.

And when they looked, they were in their parents' arms being carried through the front door. Everything was as it usually was. The wallpaper was still on the walls. Their toys were all over the floor. And the monkey masks were in a bag labelled "Zoo".

"Quick, throw them away," said Joe.

"Not in the bin, take them out of the house," pleaded Jo-Jo.

"Far away," said Joe. "Far away, so we know we're safe."

And their parents didn't know what they were talking about.

But next day, when the dustmen came, Joe and Jo-Jo made sure the bag with the masks was emptied out of their dustbin and into the truck. Then they watched it drive to the end of their street, past the newsagent's, past the milkman in his milk float, and to the edge of town.

And it wasn't until a long time later that they began to wonder if they should have kept the masks, if it might have been fun to have a jungle sometimes. But then they remembered how they had felt when they were in it, and they weren't so sure.